Families, Families, Families!

For Lulu

FAMILIES, FAMILIES, FAMILIES!
A PICTURE CORGI BOOK 978 0 552 57292 7

First published in the United States by Random House Children's Books
First published in Great Britain by Picture Corgi,
an imprint of Random House Children's Publishers UK
A Penguin Random House Company

Penguin
Random House
UK

This edition published 2015

1 3 5 7 9 10 8 6 4 2

Text copyright © Suzanne Lang, 2015
Illustrations copyright © Max Lang, 2015
Horse illustration © Rikke Asbjorn
Floral wallpaper pattern © depositphotos.com/Alexandr Labetskiy

Picture Corgi Books are published by Random House Children's Publishers UK,
61–63 Uxbridge Road, London W5 5SA

www.**randomhousechildrens**.co.uk
www.**randomhouse**.co.uk

Addresses for companies within The Random House Group Limited can be found at:
www.randomhouse.co.uk/offices.htm

THE RANDOM HOUSE GROUP Limited Reg. No. 954009

A CIP catalogue record for this book is available from the British Library.

Printed in China

Penguin Random House is committed to a sustainable future for
our business, our readers and our planet. This book is made from
Forest Stewardship Council® certified paper.

MIX
Paper from
responsible sources
FSC
www.fsc.org   FSC® C020056

Families, Families, Families!

**Suzanne Lang
& Max Lang**

PICTURE CORGI

Some children have lots of siblings.

Some children have none.

Some children have two dads.

Some have one mum.

Some children live with their grandparents . . .

and some live with an aunt.

Some children have many pets . . .

and some just have a plant!

Some children live with their father.

Some children have two mothers.

Some children are adopted.

Some have stepsisters and stepbrothers.

Some children bunk with their cousins.

Some have a mum and a pop.

Some children's parents are married.

Some children's parents are not.

So no matter if you have

a ma,

a pa,

a hog,

this llama,

ten frogs and a slug,

a cousin named Doug,

a Great-Grandma Betty
and a Great-Aunt Sue,

Uncles Hal,
Al and Sal,
and Uncle Lou, too,

one stepsis, three stepbros,
two stepmums and a prize-winning rose,

a robot butler
to serve you tea,

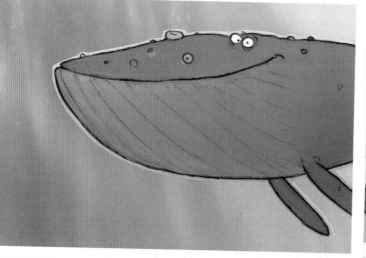

the world's biggest grandpa,

or whatever it might be . . .

. . . if you love each other,
then you are a family.